by Tracy Zimmerman
illustrated by Robert Bender

Wings
for a Day

HOUGHTON MIFFLIN BOSTON

On Monday morning, when Kenny woke up, something was different, but he wasn't sure what. He had been having another dream about flying. This time he could even picture what his wings looked like. Kenny had always wanted to fly. Just the day before, as he blew out the ten candles on his birthday cake, he had wished for wings.

As he rolled over, Kenny noticed that the T-shirt he had been sleeping in was really tight. When he stretched and flopped onto his back, he felt something peculiar underneath him.

Kenny jumped out of bed, pulled off his T-shirt, and looked in the mirror. From the front, everything looked normal—almost. Two dark shapes were barely visible over his shoulders. He turned sideways and peered behind him. What he saw just couldn't be right. He reached back to feel with his hands. It wasn't an optical illusion. He had wings!

Kenny looked again in the mirror, craning his neck to see behind him. These were no ordinary, angel-type wings. They weren't leathery bat wings, either. They were powerful-looking brown and white wings, like an osprey's. From what he could see, the tops were dark and the undersides were light.

3

When he thought about opening both wings at once—they unfurled! Kenny experimented by raising both wings, and his feet lifted off the floor. Quickly Kenny lowered the wings. He didn't want to try flying just yet. His room was too small.

Kenny moved to get dressed, but he saw right away that he had a problem. He didn't want the wings to be jammed into one of his shirts all day long. He had an idea. His mother wasn't going to like it, but maybe he could get out of the house without her noticing.

He slipped on an old flannel shirt. Then he picked up his scissors, reached around behind him, and poked holes in the shirt where his wings started. He took the shirt off and enlarged the holes. Then he worked his wings through the slits and buttoned his shirt up. His solution wasn't perfect, but it would do.

Kenny managed to get into the kitchen without being seen. He grabbed a muffin and a light jacket, called out to his parents that he was leaving, and slipped quietly out the side door.

The woods behind Kenny's house were the perfect place to try his wings. Kenny dropped his backpack and jacket on the ground and thought about fluttering his wings. He lifted off the ground a few inches and dropped back down. He tried this a few times, moving slowly from one place to another.

Next, he decided to try flying to the tree house he'd built with his brother and his father. He looked at the tree house, thought about flying . . . and the next minute he landed with a thump on the platform! He felt more timid about jumping off the platform to fly to the ground, but finally he mustered the courage. Down he flew, graceful as a bird, and then stumbled and fell in a pile of leaves. "Guess I'll have to practice landing," Kenny muttered to himself.

Glancing at his watch, Kenny realized he'd have to hurry to get to school on time. Should he walk and risk being late? Or should he take advantage of his new wings to get him to school faster? The decision was easy. Clutching his backpack and jacket to his chest, Kenny thought about taking off, raised his wings, and was airborne!

As he lifted off, Kenny hovered for a moment to get used to the odd sensation. Then he aimed himself in the direction of the school. At first he flew too close to the ground and had to dodge buildings, trees, and electrical lines. Then he aimed somewhat higher and glided smoothly through the air. He got to school in record time, before the bell.

Kenny set himself down—neatly this time—right in front of a group of his friends in the crowded schoolyard. Instantly he got everyone's attention.

When Kenny's friend Belinda calmed down, she said, "Cool! What did you do, rent some strap-on wings?"

"Nope, I just woke up this morning and found these on my back!" Kenny lifted up his shirt to show there weren't any straps. Then he flew up in the air about ten feet to demonstrate that the wings were real. This brought a round of applause from his spellbound schoolmates.

"So, do I get a ride?" Belinda challenged.

"I don't know if the wings will work for two people, but let's give it a try," said Kenny. "Hop on!"

Belinda climbed onto Kenny's shoulders. Kenny had to concentrate very hard, but slowly he lifted them both off the ground. Belinda didn't know where to put her hands, and at first she accidentally covered Kenny's eyes. They descended a moment later with a heavy thud. Kenny readjusted his balance, held on to Belinda's hands, and tried again, this time beating his wings as hard as he could. Next thing they knew, he and Belinda were perched on top of the school roof.

"Cock-a-doodle-doo!" crowed Belinda.

They swooped back to the ground. As Kenny was about to give another friend a ride, Belinda pointed to the school flag, which was flying away on the wind. Two students had been about to raise the flag when the wind tore it from their hands.

Kenny didn't even pause to think. He flew after the flag, but it kept drifting just out of reach on the breeze. Kenny beat his wings harder, maneuvered next to the flag, and grabbed it. He could hear everyone cheering as he flew back. He reattached the flag to its pole, feeling like a hero.

When the bell rang, everyone headed inside. Kenny put on his jacket. He hoped Mrs. Campana would think he was still chilly from being outdoors. But the teacher suspected that Kenny was up to some mischief and made him sit in the back of the classroom. Kenny didn't mind. He looked forward to flying some more at lunchtime.

When the bell rang for lunch, Kenny tried to be the first one out the door, but Mrs. Campana called him back. "Now, Kenny," she said, "I know it was your birthday yesterday. You must have been given a very special present that you want to share with your friends. Just make sure that you don't excite the class too much. I don't want to have to take your present away for the rest of the day or call your parents. Understand?"

Oh no! Kenny thought. He couldn't let that happen. Quickly he replied, "I understand." Mrs. Campana looked at him for a moment, nodded, and then sent him to lunch. Kenny was relieved. He decided to wait until after school to try his flying skills again.

In the gym, Mr. Wylie split the class into two teams for basketball. Kenny knew that he would get too hot with his jacket on, so he pulled the jacket off. Mr. Wylie's eyes opened wide at first as he looked at Kenny. Then his face relaxed. Kenny had never seen Mr. Wylie smile so broadly.

Early in the game, Kenny felt awkward. As usual, he hoped his teammates would pass the ball to anyone but him. Soon the other team scored. Kenny's teammate Miles stood out of bounds and tossed the ball into play. He threw the ball directly to Kenny!

At first Kenny just dribbled in a circle. He felt like a fool. It seemed like all the players on the other team were crowding around, trying to block him. Kenny stretched, trying to keep the ball away from them. Then, suddenly, Kenny was in the air. His wings! He had forgotten he could use his wings!

Kenny quickly flew above the heads of his opponents and scored a basket at the opposite end of the court. His teammates cheered.

One girl on the other team protested. "Mr. Wylie, I'd call that traveling, wouldn't you?" Mr. Wylie didn't seem to hear her.

For the rest of the game, Kenny was the most popular player. All his teammates passed the ball to him. Again and again Kenny flew to the basket and scored. At the end, the score was 42–12. His team had won.

Breathing heavily, Kenny picked up his jacket. He had thought having wings would make playing basketball a snap. He hadn't expected to feel so tired.

Kenny was thirsty, too. But on his way to the water fountain to get a drink, he saw Mr. Wylie approaching. "Great game, Kenny!" Mr. Wylie exclaimed, slapping Kenny on the back between his wings. "I don't know where you got those wings, but they'll be a terrific asset to the school team."

"The school team?" Kenny asked weakly.

"Absolutely! Don't tell me you're not interested in joining the team! We'll practice right after school. See you then."

Kenny felt uneasy about joining the basketball team, but he didn't see how he could say no to Mr. Wylie.

The next hour and a half seemed like an eternity to Kenny. He dreaded basketball practice and wished he could go home to take a nap instead. *Maybe practice will be fun,* Kenny tried to convince himself.

Reluctantly he went back to the gym after school. Mr. Wylie worked the team hard, and Kenny flew so much he felt like he was training to migrate south for the winter.

At last the practice was over. Kenny was so tired that he didn't have the energy to fly home. He walked as usual.

His mother met him at the door. She looked pale. "What's this I hear about you having wings?" she asked without saying hello. She explained that several parents of his classmates had called.

Kenny turned around so his mother could see his wings better. She put her hand to her mouth and sat down in the nearest chair. Kenny stretched out on the couch. He summarized the events of the day, starting from the moment he woke up.

"Well, I guess there's nothing much we can do about it," his mother said at last. "You'll just have to make the best of it."

That night, after doing his homework, Kenny climbed into bed early. It had been an exhausting day, and his shoulders were sore. As he closed his eyes, he realized that he didn't enjoy having wings as much as he had thought he would. He thought it might be better to swim like a fish instead.

All night long, Kenny dreamed he had the tail of a fish instead of legs. He swam so easily that he never got tired.

On Tuesday morning, when Kenny woke up, he could tell right away that his wings were gone. Still, something was different, but Kenny wasn't sure what. He tried to stretch his legs, but they felt stuck together. Suddenly Kenny remembered his dream. *Oh no*, Kenny thought. *Not again!*